Evan's Earth Day Experience

WRITTEN BY
THE ORIGINAL AUNTIE LITTER
Pat F. Mitchell

ILLUSTRATIONS BY
Jeffrey Frame

BASED ON A TRUE EVENT

The Auntie Litter® Collection

For a variety of activities and teaching tools,
visit us at www.AuntieLitter.com

Library of Congress Cataloging-in-Publication Data
Mitchell, Pat F.
Evan's Earth Day Experience/ by Pat F. Mitchell;
illustrated by Jeffrey Frame.
p. cm – (An Auntie Litter® Book #1) Summary: Evan and his new school
friends are expected to march in the big Earth Day Parade, but he
doesn't want to go. He is embarrassed, knowing his costume isn't as
good as the others. Come with Evan on his Earth Day adventure and
find out why his experience is one he will never forget.

ISBN 978-0-9668859-4-1 (pbk) / ISBN 978-0-9668859-5-8 (ebook)
Library of Congress Control Number: 2021907506

Produced in the USA.

SPECIAL THANK YOU TO:

Jeffrey Frame, illustrator, for helping me share my story.

Peggy J. Shaw, editor and advisor,
Wren Cottage Writing & Editing.

Zachary Marell, art director.

Anne Brent Wright, educational consultant and beta reader.

Ernie Eldredge for creative contributions.

Danny Tkatch and mother, Judy,
for the lyrics to "Earth! We're in it Together."

Michele Bennett, Julie Wade and LaShanna Tripp,
for encouraging me to write the book.

Jeh Jeh Pruitt and Janice Rogers,
for many Earth Day interviews.

Beverly Dracos, Laura Walker, Dr. Sonia Crist,
Jeanne Metzger, David Peaden, Vicki Wolford, E. Ashley Grund,
Michael Ferniany, and Vivian Grace Holmes, for their input and reviews.

Lana M. Holmes, Celeste M. Reeves, and Chelsey M. Edgerly,
my daughters, for all of their loving support since they were children.

Herb Mitchell, my husband,
without whom the Auntie Litter Campaign
would not have become a reality.

and…

All Pollution Patrol members, their parents, students, teachers,
chaperones, exhibitors, volunteers, sponsors, and supporters
who made Auntie Litter's Earth Day Parade and Celebration
a special event and great memory for children.

TABLE OF CONTENTS

Chapter 1

The Plan

Oh no! Evan squinted in disbelief as he saw sunshine streaming through his window. It was a beautiful spring day, but it wasn't what he wanted. He wanted rain—lots of rain—so his class field trip would be canceled. Evan didn't feel like getting dressed. All he really wanted was to stay home.

"Evan, breakfast is almost ready!" called his mother from the kitchen.

"Okay, Mom. I'll be down in a few minutes," he answered, but Evan wasn't in a hurry. He was making up a plan to be absent from school. He decided that if he didn't finish eating breakfast on time, then he'd miss the bus, which meant he wouldn't have to go on the field trip.

Yes! he thought to himself, confidently. *That's what I'll do.*

Evan stood up, breathed a big sigh of relief, and began to get dressed. After combing his hair, the fourth-grader grabbed his backpack and made his way downstairs.

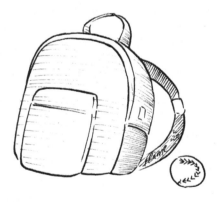

Chapter 2

TV News Blues

Evan's mother was busy making breakfast while listening to a morning news show on TV with a reporter named Jay Starr. When she saw Evan coming down the stairs, she placed a glass of milk and a bowl of oatmeal topped with blueberries on the table.

"Good morning, son," she said as he sat down. He looked at his breakfast. He was hungry, but he had to stick to his plan. He wished he could pretend to be sick and go back to his room.

"Good morning, Mom," he answered in a quiet voice, thinking this wasn't a good morning for him.

Evan slowly stirred his oatmeal. When he finally took a bite, he nearly choked, hearing Jay Starr announce: "Good morning, everyone. Today is April 22nd, and do you know what that means? It's Earth Day!"

Evan dropped his spoon, which caused an oatmeal stain on his shirt. He couldn't believe what he'd heard. He turned toward the TV as Jay Starr continued talking: "It's a perfect day for Auntie Litter's annual Earth Day Parade and Celebration."

Evan's mouth fell open in shock. They were talking about *his* field trip.

The reporter walked a couple of steps toward a dark-haired woman dressed in green, white, and blue. She wore white star earrings, a green-and-white striped shirt, and a matching headband. Her blue dress with white stars had Auntie Litter printed on the front. Evan wondered why she was dressed that way.

Jay Starr greeted the lady with a big smile and a handshake. "Good morning, Auntie Litter. I know you're happy to have perfect weather for the big parade." Then he turned the microphone toward her,

saying with a smile, "Tell us what will be happening

here at Kelly Park."

Evan's stomach tightened as he listened. Since

he was new in town, he'd never seen Auntie Litter

before. He remembered his teacher telling the class about someone named Auntie Litter, but he didn't understand who she was.

"Thanks, Jay. Happy Earth Day, everyone!" she said, smiling into the camera. "We're going to have a day filled with music, science lessons, exhibits, art, and much more. On the main stage, my Pollution Patrol and I will perform our original songs followed by a lesson on local snakes by the City Zoo."

"Wow! That sounds great, Auntie Litter," he said. "Tell us about the big parade that our TV station will air at noon."

What? Live on TV? Evan couldn't believe what he was hearing.

Auntie Litter smiled as she answered him. "Jay, hundreds of students and teachers will be dressed in colorful costumes to represent our parade theme, 'Earth! We're in it Together.' Judges will select students and school groups to receive awards for best costume, best theme, and best school spirit. The winners will be announced at our closing ceremony."

"Their creative costumes attract a crowd for this amazing parade every year," the reporter said.

Then he turned to face the camera. "So, folks, you can watch the parade on your TV live at noon, or come downtown to see it in person. Wear Earth colors —green, white, and blue—and celebrate Earth Day Auntie Litter's way!"

Chapter 3

Running Out of Excuses

Evan felt defeated. His oatmeal was cold now and he'd lost his appetite.

He remembered the day his teacher, Mrs. Bennett, read the Earth Day assignment from Auntie Litter to the class. She'd said, "The theme of the parade is 'Earth! We're in it Together.' Please think about problems that hurt our planet. Then create a costume to show one problem hurting the Earth and what we can do to protect our land, water, or air."

Suddenly, Evan's mother interrupted his thoughts.

"Is that where you're going today?" she asked, tucking a sandwich into a paper lunch bag.

"Yes," Evan answered with a sour expression. "This is going to be on TV, and my costume's not very good. Mom, can I please stay home today?"

His mother walked toward Evan calmly and said, "No, honey. I'm sure it'll be fine." She smoothed his hair. "Now, please eat your oatmeal. The bus will be at the corner any minute."

Evan wished he'd spent more time on his costume. He quickly finished breakfast and ran upstairs to change his shirt. He looked for one that had Earth colors and put it on. Then he grabbed a few colored markers out of his desk, shoved them in his backpack, and raced back downstairs. His mother was waiting with his lunch bag by the door.

She hugged him and said, "I'll see if your dad can meet me on his lunch break. Maybe we can catch the parade near his office. Enjoy your day, son."

He waved good-bye and sprinted toward the

bus stop. On the way, he saw some new friends walking from the opposite direction toward the corner, but he didn't see the trash along the sidewalk. He didn't notice the plastic bag, aluminum cans, and scraps of paper. Like many people, Evan never paid attention to litter.

Chapter 4

Creative Friends

"Hi, Evan!" called Ruthie, who was costumed to look as if she was standing in a shower. A short curtain was attached to a plastic hoop pinched with hooks. Her Earth Day message painted on the front said: "Conserve Water, Take Shorter Showers." Above Ruthie's head were strings dangling from a flower pot to look like water coming from a showerhead. She was even wearing a shower cap!

"How do you like my costume?" she asked proudly.

"What about mine?" chimed in Danny, who was dressed as a chimney. He wore black-and-gray clothing under painted cardboard in the shape of a chimney. On his head, he sported a tall hat with

charcoal gray cotton balls poofing out the top to look like smoke and soot.

He pointed one finger upward like a politician, as he said, "Be a solution to pollution!" The phrase matched the words printed on the front of his costume.

"You're funny, Danny," laughed Ruthie, "but we both know pollution's not funny. It's dangerous for all of us. Evan, where's your costume?"

Evan didn't know how to answer her. He knew his costume wasn't nearly as interesting as theirs. Just then, the school bus pulled up to the curb and the doors opened. Evan felt relieved that he did not have to answer.

Evan's friends eagerly lined up to board the bus, but he dropped to the back of the line. He wanted to be last. He kicked at the curb and thought, *I wish I could just go home.*

Chapter 5

A Sticky Mess

Evan was about to step up onto the bus when he
realized he had chewing gum on the bottom of
his shoe.

"How did that get there?" he complained to
himself. He let out a sigh looking down at the mess.

Ms. Wade, the bus driver, greeted him and then
added, "What's wrong?"

"I've got gum on the bottom of my shoe," Evan said.
"I better go home and get it cleaned up." He thought
that was a clever excuse. Before he could turn away,
though, Ms. Wade quickly grabbed her container of
cleansing wipes and came to his unwanted rescue.

"Gum is fun to chew, but not fun on your shoe!"
she said jokingly. She grabbed his shoe, cleaned the
bottom, and threw the sticky paper into a small trash
container by her driver's seat. Ms. Wade sat back
down, and cheerfully motioned for him to
come aboard.

"Thanks, Ms. Wade," he mumbled, stepping into the bus.

"I don't know why people just carelessly throw their gum on the sidewalk instead of putting it in a trash can," she said.

Evan thought about all the times he'd thrown his own gum out of the car window. He didn't think it would end up on the bottom of someone's shoe, especially his. He plopped down on the first seat behind the driver.

Ms. Wade wished she could chat a little longer with the new student because she could tell something was on his mind. Instead, she pulled the handle to close the door of the bus.

Chapter 6

Costume Check

As the bus rolled down the street, Evan pulled his costume out of his backpack. He had created a paper vest from a grocery bag.

On the front of the vest, he'd drawn four scenes of people enjoying the outdoors. The top left picture showed two people sitting under a tree in a park, and below that was a family hiking on a hillside. On the top right, Evan had drawn a man swimming in a lake, and in the fourth picture were two children playing on a beach.

Evan began to realize that his drawings showed people enjoying the environment, but they didn't show a problem affecting the Earth. Sadly, he returned the costume to his backpack and waited for the bus to stop in front of Elizabeth Fern Elementary School.

Chapter 7

Earth Day Ready

"Happy Earth Day!" exclaimed Mrs. Bennett, as her students entered the classroom. She was holding green cloth tote bags.

"Now remember, friends, this is a litter-free event. Auntie Litter has given each of us a tote bag as an Earth Day gift to collect information from the exhibitors," she said. "Carrying these will also help us keep the park clean." She gave one to each student and then asked, "Is everyone ready? It's almost time to board the buses."

Evan looked around the room at all the colorful costumes. His new friends were talking and laughing while admiring each other's creations. He was relieved no one noticed he wasn't wearing one.

Chapter 8

Perfect Park

It was almost 9 a.m. when the three buses from the school pulled up to Kelly Park downtown. Mr. Ireland, the principal, and some parent volunteers stepped off the first bus and began unloading drink coolers and picnic blankets.

The sun was shining brightly, and Evan could see huge oak trees with their branches swaying gently in the breeze. Flowers lined four walkways to the center of the park where a large fountain sprayed water gracefully about six feet high in a silent rhythm. The lawn looked freshly mowed and the park was clean.

"What a beautiful place to spend Earth Day," Evan whispered to himself.

As Evan followed his teacher, he could see exhibitors setting up tents to shade their tables. He saw ladies folding Earth Day T-shirts and a man arranging microphones and speakers on the stage.

Mrs. Bennett found a place under a big tree to spread out picnic blankets for their group. After everything was organized, she turned to her class and said, "Friends, get your tote bags, line up, and follow me. Let's celebrate Earth Day!"

Chapter 9

Fun and Games

Evan's class walked to the first exhibit where people were making paper hats from newspapers. "This is one way we can reuse papers," explained the exhibitor, "and if we recycle them, they will become *new* newspapers." He pointed to a drawing on a poster board of how newsprint can be recycled to become new paper. He finished by giving each person a booklet with recycling facts to take home.

Evan and his friends had a blast making newspaper hats. Danny pretended to be a ship's captain and Ruthie posed like a movie star. Evan's first hat was too big, but he was delighted his second hat was a perfect fit. No one wanted to go, but Mrs. Bennett said it was time to move on.

At the next exhibit, tables were covered with socks, strings, and clean plastic milk jugs. "You see, boys and girls, you can make a game from things you use at home," said a man in a flowered shirt as he held up a gallon container. "Auntie Litter calls this game Ball in a Jug."

He pointed to a line on the jug, and said, "Please ask an adult to cut the bottom section off below the handle to create a scoop. Then make a ball by folding two old socks together. Next, tie a string around the sock ball and connect it to the scoop handle."

Class chaperones helped students cut the bottoms off milk jugs and roll socks into balls. Then, the students began swinging their sock balls into the air and catching them in the scoops.

"When we recycle heavy plastic like this, companies can create many things like picnic tables, park benches, boat docks, and fences, instead of using wood from trees," the man informed them.

Evan had never really thought much about reusing things or recycling, and he sure didn't know he could make a game from a milk jug. He put the game pieces and directions in his tote bag.

Just then, Mrs. Bennett saw Auntie Litter and her Pollution Patrol lining up on stage. "Friends, Auntie Litter's show is starting. Let's go!" She quickly arranged her students in single file to make their way through the crowd.

Chapter 10

Singing with Meaning

Mrs. Bennett led her class to the front of the stage. Evan couldn't believe he was standing right in front of Auntie Litter. Behind her were kids wearing blue shorts and white T-shirts that said *Pollution Patrol* in green letters. Ruthie told him two of the performers were from their school.

Evan grinned and said, "That's so cool."

Members of the Pollution Patrol began singing and dancing to "Auntie Litter's 3R Rap." The crowd grew wild with excitement, saying the 3Rs as loud as they could: "Reuse! Reduce Waste! Recycle!" Evan was having so much fun with his new friends that he'd forgotten about his costume.

For the next song, Auntie Litter asked the audience to repeat the chorus and follow her dance steps to "Earth! We're in it Together." As Evan sang along, he thought about the meaning of these important words:

Earth! We're in it together
Forever and ever.
Saving our water, land, and air.
This is our planet to share.

Chapter 11

Hooray for the Hero

After visiting each exhibit and watching the science show, Mrs. Bennett led her students back to their picnic blankets for lunch. Evan noticed two big dogs playfully chasing each other. Within minutes, the first dog knocked over a large trash can that started to roll. Trash was flying everywhere.

"Oh no," he shouted. "Litter!"

Evan quickly sprang into action to keep the park clean. Mrs. Bennett and others saw Evan chasing the trash can as it rolled toward the park fountain, flinging garbage along the way. They jumped up to help him, doing their best to grab paper cups, plastic bags, napkins, and other items whirling in the breeze.

Kids were chasing trash and the dogs were chasing each other. There was so much chaos that everyone in the park was looking their way.

After a while, they put all the trash back in the can. Everyone could see Mrs. Bennett's hair was a mess, her face was red, and she looked exhausted.

Auntie Litter was delighted to see this remarkable Earth-saving act and walked over to thank everyone for their efforts. She turned toward Evan and complimented him on being proactive.

"I'm glad to help," Evan proudly stated. "I've learned so much today about our planet and how each person can make a difference." Then he added, sadly, "Auntie

Litter, I just wish I had made a better costume for the Earth Day Parade."

She leaned down to look at him face-to-face and kindly replied, "Evan, it's not the costume on the outside that's important; it's what's in your heart that counts. I can tell you care about our Earth. You proved that just now by keeping the park litter-free and beautiful."

"I do care, Auntie Litter," he replied with a smile.

Chapter 12

Working Together

The students cleaned their hands and enjoyed their lunches. Evan suddenly had a brainstorm. He realized that some of the items he'd just used at lunch could be reused for his costume.

"Ruthie, I've got an idea. Can you lend me four shower hooks for my costume?"

She could tell he was bubbling over with excitement, so she quickly reached over to unclamp a few hooks she could do without. "Here you go," she said, handing them to Evan. "Do you need my help?"

Danny added cheerfully, "I'll help too."

Evan wanted his costume to show how litter is an everyday problem hurting the Earth. So, together, the three friends took used items from Evan's lunch bag and clamped them to his paper vest. They attached a paper napkin to the ground in the park scene and an empty fruit cup to the hiking trail. Next, they clipped a small, empty plastic water bottle to the lakeshore, and connected a chip bag to the beach picture.

Finally, Evan pulled out markers from his backpack and drew a big picture of Auntie Litter on the back of his vest with these words:

In a flash, Evan put on the decorated vest and topped the costume with his newspaper hat. He proudly announced to his friends, "Now, I'm ready to march in the Earth Day Parade!"

Chapter 13

Surprise for Evan

Hundreds of spectators lined the sidewalks waiting for the big parade to start at noon. Police officers blocked off streets from oncoming traffic as school groups went to their assigned parade locations.

While Mrs. Bennett organized her students in rows to march in the parade, Auntie Litter walked through the lineup to greet the marchers and admire the costume creations. She spotted Evan with his class, and said, "What a great costume, Evan! How would you like to lead the parade with me?"

Grinning from ear-to-ear, he answered, "That would be awesome! Can Ruthie and Danny come too?"

"Sure," she answered, happily. "As long as it's okay with your teacher."

Mrs. Bennett was thrilled for her students to be given this honor. She beamed with pride as she watched them walk with Auntie Litter to the front of the line.

Chapter 14

Lesson Learned

Leading the Earth Day Parade was the H. Joseph High School Band. The band's music could be heard several blocks away—rolling sounds from small to large drums, clashing cymbals, and trumpets blaring in perfect harmony.

This pollution-free parade had no cars or trucks. Everyone was walking, marching, dancing, skating, riding bicycles, and pushing strollers or wheelchairs. There were brightly colored costumes featuring flowers, trees, fish, ocean waves, wildlife, recycled

robots, and more. Voices of teachers and students filled the air with chants of *"Save our environment! Reuse, Reduce waste, Recycle!"* and *"Be a litter quitter!"*

A little farther down the wide city street, Evan spotted his parents waving to him. They were surprised to see him at the front of the parade with Auntie Litter. Evan waved back and was happy that he didn't stay home and miss everything today.

As they turned the first corner of Second Avenue, Evan was amazed at how far down the street the big parade went. He turned toward Auntie Litter and said, "This is the most exciting day of my life! I wish every day could be Earth Day."

"Evan, every day *is* Earth Day!" she replied with a twinkle in her eye.

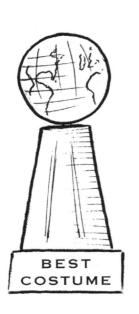

BEST
COSTUME

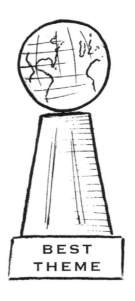

BEST
THEME

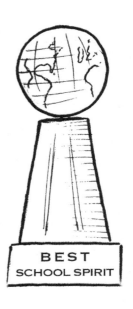

BEST
SCHOOL SPIRIT

Chapter 15

The Special Award

Following the parade, Evan's class relaxed on the picnic blankets with cold drinks and snacks. Ruthie, Danny, and Evan were having fun sharing their stories about what it was like to lead the big parade.

"I saw TV cameras while we were marching. Do you think we'll be on the news tonight?" asked Danny.

Ruthie was quick to reply, "I don't know, but I waved and smiled just in case."

Just then, they heard the announcement that it was time for the Earth Day Awards. The beautiful trophies were lined up on a table next to Auntie Litter. The school groups listened carefully to the names being called in each category. One-by-one, winners went up to receive their awards and pose for pictures with Auntie Litter.

Auntie Litter looked around at all the colorful costumes and held up the last trophy. She announced, "Our first-place winner for Best Costume goes to Ruthie from Elizabeth Fern Elementary!" Everyone from her school screamed and cheered when they heard Ruthie's shower costume had won.

Ruthie was surprised and very happy. "Thank you, Auntie Litter," she said, as she held up her trophy and posed for the camera.

Chapter 16

Every Day is Earth Day

On the bus ride home, Evan thought about the beautiful park and what Auntie Litter had said about every day being Earth Day. As he looked through the window, he noticed trash littering the streets, even though trash cans were nearby. And he saw old garage sale signs and other advertisements tacked onto utility poles.

As he stepped off the bus at his corner, Evan realized litter was a problem even in his own neighborhood. He wondered why he had never noticed it before.

He reached in his tote bag, took out an empty sandwich wrapper to protect his hand, and began to pick up trash scattered on and off the sidewalk.

He hummed the tune and began singing the words he'd learned that day:

Earth! We're in it together
Forever and ever.
Saving our water, land, and air.
This is our planet to share.

When he got to his front doorsteps, Evan turned and looked back at his neighborhood, which was just a little bit cleaner. He smiled and proudly whispered to himself, "Yes, Auntie Litter, every day *is* Earth Day."

Celebrating Earth Day

Reuse

Auntie Litter's Way

Recycle

Reduce

 Visit us at www.AuntieLitter.com

About the Author

Pat Mitchell is the founder of Auntie Litter, Inc., a national nonprofit organization dedicated to providing environmental education to the general public, particularly children. To spread her message about protecting the environment, she portrayed the character of Auntie Litter to "do for the environment what Uncle Sam has done for patriotism." Under her leadership, numerous programs and materials have been developed, which gained national recognition: President George H. Bush *Take Pride in America Award*, DAR *Conservation Award*, Girl Scouts *Woman of Distinction Award*, President Bill Clinton *Point of Light*, and the U.S. Environmental Protection Agency *Clean Air Excellence Award* for *Education and Outreach*. The Auntie Litter Campaign was covered by many media outlets, including *CNN Headline News*, *ABC News*, and *USA Today*. Ms. Mitchell credits her inspiration as a gift from God.

About the Illustrator

Jeffrey Frame has always enjoyed storytelling. He's been creating characters and drawing comic strips since high school. His illustrations are the highlight of the children's book *Seagulls, Sandcastles & Angels of Blue*, a delightful story about a family of seagulls who take a trip to see an airshow. After many years of creating comics, he completed his first book, *The Smiley Face Commandos: Comic Strip Collection*, a humorous, action-adventure about a crime-fighting trio of heroes. Mr. Frame is also an avid independent filmmaker and has written and directed more than ten short films, most of which can be found at BigLagoonMedia.com.

Fun Pages For You!

Song Lyrics ▶ YouTube
Earth Day Activities
What Do You Remember?
Grow Your Vocabulary
and
A SNEAK PREVIEW
Auntie Litter's Recycling Rescue!

Earth, We're in It Together

CHORUS
Earth, We're in it Together
Forever and ever.
Saving our water, land and air.
This is our planet to share!

We need clean air around us all,
land to walk on and waterfalls;
but the world is changing day by day,
listen to what we say!
One by one, we can spread the news
about how to stop pollution blues!
Together we're reaching out to you
to help us save the Earth.

Repeat Chorus

Imagine our world clean and litter-free
from the ocean to the sky;
Join our hands, share the vision we can see.
Let's begin by taking pride!

Repeat Chorus (twice)

Ending:
Together we can show we care.
This is our Earth to share!
We're in it together!

 YouTube

Go to www.YouTube.com/AuntieLitter

Auntie Litter's 3R Rap

Chorus:
Reuse, Reduce Waste, Recycle
(Say 3 times)

You look like a real go-getter!
Come on help your Auntie Litter!
Chorus.

There are others to consider; Think it over, Don't Litter!
Repeat Chorus.

Stash your trash; Don't throw it down.
Take pride in your hometown.
Repeat Chorus.

Ask your friends to not be bitter. Get them to be a Litter Quitter.
Repeat Chorus.

We won't give up. We won't give in. We want our world clean again.
Repeat Chorus.

Share the vision we can see, America Litter Free!
Repeat Chorus.

You can save our landfill space.
Reuse, recycle, and reduce your waste!
Repeat Chorus.

Please remember what we've said.
Keep the 3-Rs in your head!
Repeat Chorus.

Say what?
Repeat Chorus.

Don't forget!
Repeat Chorus.

One more time!
Repeat Chorus.

Let's start now!

Go to www.YouTube.com/AuntieLitter

It's time to get creative with

EARTH DAY ACTIVITIES

Auntie's Ball in a Jug

Paper Hats

Sand Sculpture in a Jar

Build a Bird Feeder

Checkers

Tic-Tac-Toe Game

Auntie's Ball in a Jug

This project is hours of REUSABLE fun. You will need:

- An empty one-gallon plastic milk jug
- An old sock
- An old stocking
- A two-foot piece of string
- Scissors

Cut off the bottom of the milk jug starting just below the handle, so that it looks like a big scoop. Put the sock in the stocking and tie it in a knot to form a ball. Attach one end of the string to the ball and the other to the jug handle. Now try to catch the ball with the jug. Or... you and a friend can remove the string and toss the ball from scoop to scoop.

Paper Hats

Make hats out of newspaper!

Fold a sheet of newspaper in half.

Bring the corners down until they meet.

Fold up the bottom edge on top and then turn over and fold up the other bottom edge in the opposite direction.

Staple or tape the corners.

Decorate with paints or construction paper scraps.

Sand Sculpture in a Jar

You will need:

- Small, clean baby food jar
- Dry sand (sugar or oats will work too)
- Box of colored chalk
- Plates

You'll be coloring the sand with the chalk, so put a small amount of sand on each plate- one for each of the selected colors. Rub one color of chalk through the sand in one plate. It will start to color the sand. Do the same for each color.

With your jar, start making layers of colored sand, a little at a time. Keep doing this until you have completely filled the jar at the top. If it is not totally packed, the sand will shift. Be sure to cap the jar tightly. You can paint or decorate the jar lids too.

Build a Bird Feeder

3 Easy Steps

1. Use a 3-liter plastic bottle. Ask an adult to help you with this part. Cut 4 holes on the sides of the bottle (from which the birds will feed).

2. Make small slits (like an X), 1 inch under the holes, and slide a dowel through them. Use an eye screw through the cap of the bottle or a nylon cord looped to hang.

3. Fill your feeder with birdseed and hang outside near a window.

Checkers

Supplies Needed:
- one clean pizza box
- 24 plastic milk bottle tops.
- markers
- paint
- ruler

Measure and mark the inside of the pizza box with 2" x 2" squares. Color them in a checkerboard pattern using two colors of markers. Make two different colored sets of twelve game pieces out of the plastic milk bottle tops. If necessary, paint the tops.

Tic-Tac-Toe Game

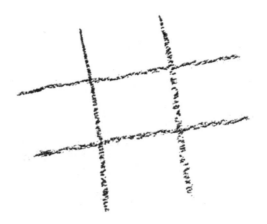

Supplies Needed:

- an empty, clean cereal box
- 12 plastic milk bottle tops
- markers
- ruler
- safety scissors

Cut out the back panel of the box for the game board. Draw a three by three game board with two-inch squares on the inside panel. Paint two sets of six tops to be used for game pieces.

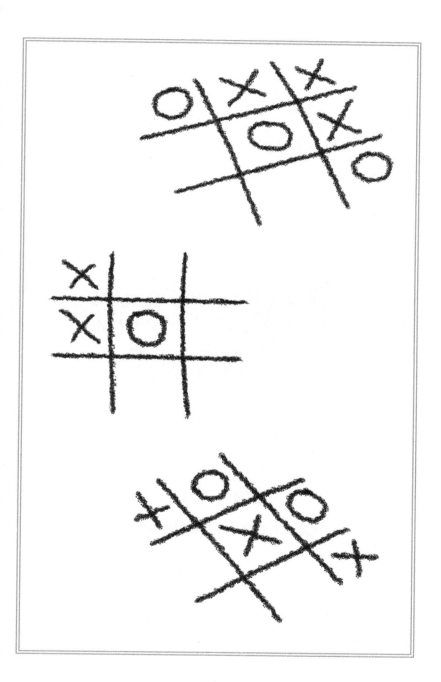

**Earn Your
Pollution Patrol Points!**

Book Challenges

What Do You Remember?

page 86

How well did you pay attention to the story? Take the reading comprehension quiz.

Grow Your Vocabulary

page 94

Do you know the words in the list? If not, look them up in a dictionary to grow your vocabulary.

WHAT DO YOU REMEMBER?

How many questions, below, can you answer, either from what you remember or from looking back in the chapters? The answers are on page 90.

Questions

Chapter 1

a. What was Evan hoping to see when he woke up?

b. What was his plan?

c. What grade is Evan in?

Chapter 2

a. Who was speaking with the reporter on TV?

b. What is special about April 22?

c. Where were Evan and his classmates going on their field trip?

Chapter 3

a. What was the theme of the parade?

b. What colors were on the shirt that Evan wore to school?

c. What did Evan fail to notice along the sidewalk as he ran to the bus stop?

Chapter 4

a. What was Ruthie's Earth Day costume message?

b. What was Danny's Earth Day costume message?

c. Why didn't Evan want to show his costume?

Chapter 5

a. When Evan arrived at the bus, what did he find on his shoe?

b. Who is Ms. Wade?

c. Where should we put gum when we are through with it?

Chapter 6

a. What did Evan use to create his costume?

b. How many scenes did he draw on his costume?

c. What was part of Evan's assignment that was missing from his drawings?

Chapter 7

a. What was Mrs. Bennett giving to each student from Auntie Litter?

b. What was the purpose of the tote bags?

c. Was Evan wearing his costume in the classroom?

Chapter 8

a. What time did the buses arrive at Kelly Park?

b. What was in the center of the park?

c. What did Evan say when he saw Kelly Park?

Chapter 9

a. What did the children create from newspapers?

b. Name one thing that can be made from recycling heavy plastic.

c. What did Evan put in his tote bag when leaving the exhibit?

Chapter 10

a. Who were the performers on stage with Auntie Litter?

b. What are the 3Rs?

c. Finish this line in the song: "This is our planet to

_____."

Chapter 11

a. What knocked over the trash can?

b. What did Evan do when the trash can overturned?

c. Complete Auntie Litter's sentence about Evan's costume:

"It's what's in your _____ that counts."

Chapter 12

a. What did Evan borrow from Ruthie?

b. What did he want to show on his costume that is hurting the Earth?

c. Whose picture did Evan draw on the back of his costume?

Chapter 13

a. What did Auntie Litter ask Evan?

b. What did Evan ask Auntie Litter?

c. Why did Evan want to include Ruthie and Danny in his special moment?

Chapter 14

a. What made the parade pollution-free?

b. Name one group of costumes worn by students in the parade.

c. Were Evan's parents at the parade?

Chapter 15

a. What did Danny see while marching in the parade?

b. What was Auntie Litter giving to the winners?

c. Ruthie won first place for Best _____.

Chapter 16

a. What did Evan see through the bus window on the way home?

b. What did he decide to do for his neighborhood?

c. What did Evan say when he reached his front doorsteps?

"Yes, Auntie Litter, every day is

_____ _____."

WHAT DO YOU REMEMBER?

Answers

Chapter 1

a. Rain

b. To miss the bus and be absent from school.

c. Fourth grade

Chapter 2

a. Auntie Litter

b. It's Earth Day!

c. Auntie Litter's Earth Day Parade

Chapter 3

a. Earth, we're in it together

b. Earth Day colors—green, white and blue

c. Trash or litter

Chapter 4

a. Conserve Water, Take Shorter Showers

b. Be a Solution to the Pollution

c. He didn't think his costume was as interesting as theirs

Chapter 5

a. Someone threw it on the ground

b. The bus driver

c. The trash can

Chapter 6

a. A paper grocery bag

b. Four

c. A problem hurting the earth

Chapter 7

a. Tote bags

b. To collect information and keep the park clean

c. No

Chapter 8

a. 9 a.m.

b. A fountain

c. Evan said, "What a beautiful place to spend Earth Day."

Chapter 9

a. Hats

b. Picnic tables, park benches, boat docks, and fences

c. Game pieces and directions

Chapter 10

a. The Pollution Patrol

b. Reuse, Reduce Waste, Recycle

c. Share

Chapter 11

a. A dog

b. Jumped up to catch the trash

c. Heart

Chapter 12

a. Shower hooks

b. Litter

c. Auntie Litter

Chapter 13

a. To lead the parade

b. If Ruthie and Danny could lead it too

c. They are his friends

Chapter 14

a. No cars or trucks

b. Flowers, trees, fish, ocean waves, wildlife, or recycled robots

c. Yes

Chapter 15

a. TV Cameras

b. Trophies or awards

c. Costume

Chapter 16

a. Trash and signs on poles

b. Pick up litter

c. Earth Day

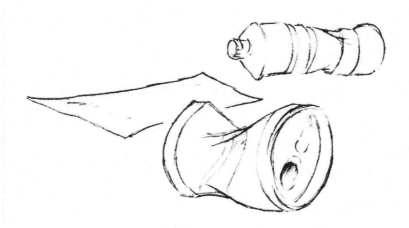

Auntie Litter: Evan's Earth Day Experience

GROW YOUR VOCABULARY

How many of these words do you know?

Experience	Defeated
Plan	Interrupted
Squinted	Expression
Disbelief	Costume
Streaming	Sprinted
Confidently	Aluminum
Pretend	Attention
Continued	Litter
Celebration	Attached
Handshake	Dangling
Microphone	Excitement
Station	Politician
Attract	Sollution

Pollution	Section
Dangerous	Informed
Excuse	Arranged
Carelessly	Audience
Complained	Whirling
Exclaimed	Chaos
Collect	Remarkable
Exhibitors	Complimented
Admiring	Proactive
Creations	Brainstorm
Relieved	Connected
Microphones	Assigned
Reuse	Extremely
Reduce	Announcement
Waste	Advertisements
Recycle	Scattered

Auntie Litter's Recycling Rescue

WRITTEN BY
THE ORIGINAL AUNTIE LITTER
Pat F. Mitchell

Preview

The Auntie Litter® Collection

Chapter 1

Evan was eager to go outside for recess. He'd completed his reading lesson and was putting his book in his desk when he heard his teacher, Mrs. Bennett, announce in a bubbly voice, "Friends, I have some exiting news! Auntie Litter is coming this afternoon to give our school a program on how to protect our environment."

Evan turned, wide-eyed, toward Ruthie and Danny. "Do you think she'll remember us leading the Earth Day Parade with her?"

"I hope so," Ruthie answered. "Leading that parade was awesome!"

"Let's ask Mrs. Bennett if our class can find seats up front in the auditorium. Maybe she'll see us," Danny chimed in.

Auntie Litter had chosen Evan, Ruthie and Danny to lead the Earth Day Parade with her in April. The event impressed them so much that the three friends made a pact to help Auntie Litter protect the Earth.

They'd agreed to meet every Saturday morning at

Evan's house for litter patrol. Wearing rubber gloves and carrying plastic bags for litter pick-up, the three friends walked along the sidewalks removing cans, bottles, paper, and other things that didn't belong on the ground.

Sitting at his desk, Evan started thinking back to one morning a few weeks earlier when they were busy picking up litter. Their neighbor, Mrs. Gabriel, spoke with them.

"Good morning, neighbors," greeted Mrs. Gabriel. "Are you on litter patrol again? I've seen you coming by each week to clean up trash that people carelessly drop on our sidewalks and yards. Thank you for keeping our neighborhood clean."

"You're welcome, Mrs. Gabriel!" the three said together, with smiles.

"We're helping Auntie Litter protect the Earth," added Ruthie.

Evan suddenly remembered a line from "Auntie

Litter's 3R Rap," a song they learned at the Earth Day Celebration. He blurted out in rap style:

Stash your trash,
Don't throw it down,
Take pride in your hometown!

Together, they chanted the chorus:

Reuse, Reduce Waste, Recycle!

"Mrs. Gabriel, did you know our country spends millions of dollars each year paying companies to remove litter off our streets and highways?" asked Ruthie. "My dad said if people wouldn't litter, this money could be used to fix or build new schools, bridges, roads, and other things we need."

"Your father's right, Ruthie," said Mrs. Gabriel. She loved their enthusiasm and asked if she could help. She went inside her home to get a pair of gloves and a sunhat. She was happy to be a part of something special for her community.

After just three weeks, the group noticed there was less litter and neighbors were keeping their yards clean and planting flowers. It was obvious that Old Oak residents were taking pride in their community, and the weekly clean-up campaign was making a difference.

Evan was wishing a recycling program was available for the items they'd had collected when he heard Mrs. Bennett call, "Time for recess!"

Dear Friends,

I hope you enjoyed
Evan's Earth Day Experience
and will always remember:

Every Day is Earth Day!

Please visit Auntie Litter's website for
more fun at www.AuntieLitter.com

Love,
Auntie Litter

Reuse • Reduce Waste • Recycle

Made in the USA
Coppell, TX
23 April 2022

76949880R00059